Tom Percival

Little Legends

THE STORY TREE

Tom Percival grew up in a remote and beautiful part of south Shropshire. It was so remote that he lived in a small caravan without mains electricity or any sensible form of heating. He thinks he's probably one of the few people in his peer group to have learned to read by gas lamp.

Having established a career as a picture-book author and illustrator, Little Legends is Tom's first chapter-book series for young readers. The idea for Little Legends was developed by Tom with Made in Me, a digital studio exploring new ways for technology and storytelling to

M̲ ̲KS

This book is dedicated to Rory Kellehar Greener
(and his mum, Rachel, who helped make
Little Legends happen. Thank you!)

First published 2017 by Macmillan Children's Books
an imprint of Pan Macmillan
20 New Wharf Road, London N1 9RR
Associated companies throughout the world
www.panmacmillan.com

ISBN 978-1-5098-4217-9

1 3 5 7 9 8 6 4 2

A CIP catalogue record for this book is available from the British Library.

Printed and bound by CPI Group (UK) Ltd, Croydon CR0 4YY

Contents

1

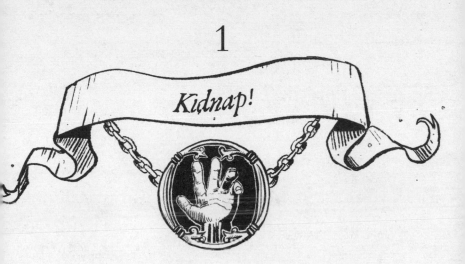

Kidnap!

*T*he air was cold, and the moon shone high up in the sky, like a thin slice of apple that had been painted silver. Or maybe it was more like a silver slither of sliced banana? Or perhaps some other piece of silver-coloured fruit? Who knows! Anyway, the moon was *definitely* there and the air was *definitely* cold as Jack crept around the edge of Market Square in Tale Town, darting from shadow to shadow as he tried to avoid Mayor Fitch's guards. He was halfway across the square when a patrol marched out of a side alley and turned in his direction. Ever since Mayor Fitch had announced that Tale Town was at war with the trolls, the whole place had been on lockdown.

Jack panicked and threw himself into a bush.

'WhAaaat?' protested the bush.

'Shhhhhhhhh!' hissed Jack.

'WhaAaaaaaat?!' repeated the bush angrily.

'I *can't* find another hiding place!' whispered Jack. 'The guards are coming! Besides, there's *plenty* of room.'

'Whaaat...' muttered the bush, which sounded like it was *maybe* agreeing, but wasn't very happy about it.

Jack waited until all the guards had left the square, then burst out of the bush, followed by a cross-looking hen.

'Whaaaaat!' squawked the hen quietly.

'Well, how was *I* to know you were hiding in there, Betsy?' asked Jack. 'It's *really* dark and you're kind of *small*. Did you see where Red and Wolfie went?'

Betsy shook her head and squawked **'WhaAaat'** again.

Now, talking to a hen is one thing, but having it reply is most definitely unusual. Then again, Tale Town is a very unusual place, where stories grow on trees, eggs can climb up walls (*and* fall off them) and hens can talk. Admittedly the only word Betsy can actually *say* is 'what', but even so, Jack always knows what she means and they more or less muddle through.

'Psssssssst!' hissed a lamp post above them. Jack looked up. A talking lamp post *too*? Things were getting ridiculous. Then he saw his friend Red clinging to the top of it. She grinned at him, swinging down to the ground.

'Come on!' she whispered. 'I could see Wolfie from up there. He's waiting for us on the path to the beach.'

Red and Jack ran through the town without any more trouble and scrambled over the huge wall that Mayor Fitch was building all around Tale Town. It wasn't finished yet but when it *was*, there would only be one gateway leading into the town, and *that* would be heavily guarded. It would have a drawbridge, a portcullis, vats of boiling oil ready to be poured out at a moment's notice and a large, golden statue of Mayor Fitch.

The statue
wasn't going
to help with
the guarding,
of course, but
Fitch liked gold
and he liked himself.
So there *was* going
to be a gold statue, and
anyone who disagreed would
find themselves banished. There were
posters everywhere saying that the wall
was going to keep the trolls out. But it
was *also* starting to make the townsfolk
feel like they were being kept in.

The main reason for this massive wall
was to protect the Story Tree, which
was the one thing that Mayor Fitch

prized above anything else. Any stories that were told near it would grow on its branches, appearing as a shiny gold or silver leaf. To experience any of the stories on there, all you had to do was touch the leaf and you would be transported *inside* the story. It was Tale Town's greatest asset and Mayor Fitch thought that the trolls were trying to steal it. Well, that's what he was saying, but Jack and the others knew it was a lie. The trolls had actually helped to plant the Story Tree hundreds of years ago when trolls and humans *used* to live together in peace – until Mayor Fitch's family had changed all that, by trying to keep the trolls out.

Now trolls and humans were mortal enemies, and ever since Jack and his friends had helped a captured troll child to escape from Mayor Fitch, *they* had become outlaws and all their parents had been banished to Far Far Away. Jack and his friends had to live in a hideout in the woods just outside of Tale Town with a small green monkey called Alphege and a group of super-intelligent gorillas.

'I still can't believe that Fitch is cutting whichever stories he doesn't like off the Story Tree!' said Red, shaking her head. 'That's just *wrong*!'

Jack nodded. 'I know! Still, that's how he's able to get everyone in Tale Town to believe him. As long as he only tells *his* side of the story, then nobody knows any different!'

They heard the secret signal that Wolfie had insisted they use to communicate – a wolf's howl. Betsy had suggested that they should use a hen's squawk instead but she had been overruled and was a bit grumpy about it. Everyone was used to that, though –

Betsy was a bit grumpy about most things.

'I *still* don't know why we needed to do this in the middle of the night!' muttered Wolfie, anxiously stroking the soft, lavender-scented fur of his tail. 'It's *so* creepy. I mean, there could be *anything* out there!' He peered around at the tall dark cliffs unhappily. 'Couldn't we just have come down here on a nice sunny afternoon instead?'

Red patted Wolfie's arm. 'We have to go through town to get down to the beach, and we can't be seen in town now we're outlaws! Now *come on* – Lily will be waiting for us.'

Lily was a Sea Witch. Well a *junior* Sea Witch. Actually she was *training* to be a junior Sea Witch. To be perfectly honest, she wasn't really very good at being a Sea Witch, but that was no fault of her own. Being a Sea Witch *usually* meant that you had to do all sorts of horrible things to people and sell them spells that wouldn't really work — but Lily was *far* too nice for all that sort of thing and tried to help Jack and his friends whenever she could.

Red, Jack, Betsy and Wolfie tiptoed down to the beach and Wolfie howled out the secret signal. The water rippled and Lily's head rose slowly up out of the sea. When she saw Jack and the others she gave them a huge smile and cast the spell that would carry them all safely down to her underwater cave.

The water near Jack started snaking through the air, twirling towards them like ribbons, when a sudden shout distracted Lily. The curling strands of water paused for a moment as six of Mayor Fitch's guards came running across the beach towards them.

'Hurry up!' yelled Red to Lily and ran waist deep into the sea, grabbing Betsy and ushering Jack and Wolfie forward. The spell was building up

to its full strength and the water was towering around them in a column, making a tunnel that would lead down to Lily's cave. Just as they started to slide down the watery walls, two strong arms reached in and grabbed Wolfie's shoulders. The arms pulled him back as Red, Jack and Betsy slid away, watching helplessly as they tumbled down to the depths of the ocean.

2

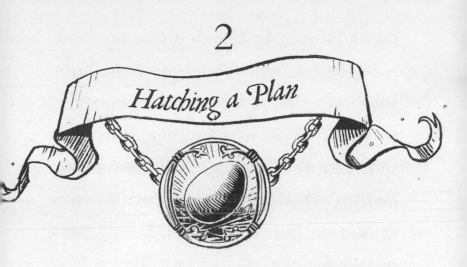

Hatching a Plan

*W*here's Wolfie?' asked Lily as the bubbles cleared and Red, Jack and Betsy were left bobbing up and down in the water of her cave.

'He's gone,' said Jack quietly. 'Fitch's guards took him.'

'What?' gasped Lily. 'We've *got* to get him back! Can you imagine Wolfie being locked up in prison? No scented candles? No fur-dryer? No fabric conditioner? He'll *never* make it!'

'*Of course* we have to rescue him,' said Jack. 'It's just one more impossible thing we've got to do, along with all the *other* impossible things . . . Like freeing Anansi's uncle and mum from the magic crystal on Hurrilan's staff. Like getting all our parents back to Tale Town. Like proving that Fitch has been lying about the trolls. Sometimes it just feels like he's going to win and there's *nothing* we can do about it.' Jack's shoulders sagged as he floated sadly in the water.

Betsy swam over, grabbed his jumper and squawked **'WhaAaaat!'** in a *very* determined way.

'Betsy's right,' exclaimed Red. 'You've got to get a grip, Jack! We *can't* give up. *Yes*, Fitch has taken away our homes, our parents and our access to Greentop's Cafe's delicious selection of musical milkshakes, but he can NEVER take away our HOPE!'

As she spoke, stirring orchestral music started playing in the background and Jack looked around confused until he saw Lily floating next to an old record player. The music

grew louder as Red continued – she liked making speeches.

'We'll make sure *everyone* can record their stories on the Story Tree – man, woman, troll, goat or incy-wincy spider! We will *NEVER* give up. Even if Fitch captures *all* of us. Even if he forces us to eat cold rice pudding and . . .'

'WhaAaa Aaaaaat!' interrupted Betsy, looking unsure, and the music suddenly stopped.

'Well, I'm sure it won't come to *that*,' replied Red. 'But the point is, we don't give up. *Right?*' She looked round at her friends, who all nodded. Even Jack seemed to have perked up a bit.

'OK!' he exclaimed. 'We keep going. It's not like things can get any worse!'

There was a loud chime from the magic mirror that Red kept in her pocket. She flipped the little case open, and a second later her reflection faded away and was replaced by their friend Quartz, looking pale and worried. Quartz was the troll child that Red and her friends had rescued from the Tale Town stocks. After they had managed to get him back to his family, Quartz had given Red a magic mirror so they could still speak to each other, even if they were hundreds of miles apart.

'There's going to be a troll attack!' whispered Quartz's reflection without even saying hello. He looked anxiously from side to side before he added, 'On Tale Town!'

'*What?* But *how*?' gasped Jack, leaning in close to the mirror. 'What about the Moonstone defences? Trolls can't get past it – it makes them sick, doesn't it?'

'Well, yeah,' continued Quartz, 'but I think they've found a way round it. That's all I know – Hurrilan's planning an attack on Tale Town and he's sending the whole army – this is going to be *big*!'

'When?' asked Red.

'Tomorrow, at dawn,' replied Quartz. 'We're coming down from the north . . .'

'What?' spluttered Jack. 'What do you mean, "*We're* coming down"?'

'Hurrilan's bringing *everyone*, all the trolls that were hiding in the Secret Mountain. Like I said, this is going to be big!' There was a noise in the background and Quartz froze, his face going even paler. '*Got to go*,' he hissed, and then faded away until the mirror was just showing Red's reflection again.

'OK . . .' said Jack slowly. 'I guess I was wrong.'

'About what?' asked Red.

'Well, things *can* get worse . . .' said Jack. 'They just have.'

Ten minutes later they were no closer to working out what to do – about any of it. Everything seemed hopeless. If Hurrilan *did* attack Tale Town, then they would *never* be able to explain that it was Mayor Fitch who had created this whole mess just to get more power!

'Wait a minute!' exclaimed Jack. 'What if we went back in time and made Fitch decide *NOT* to become Mayor of Tale Town but

to become . . . I don't know . . . a *hairdresser* instead?'

'Hmmm . . .' said Red, with a look that seemed to say, '*That's one of the most ridiculous ideas I've ever heard in my whole life.*'

Jack's cheeks flushed.

'**WhaAaaAaaaaat!**' added Betsy, and Jack shrugged grumpily.

'Of *course* I don't know how we'd do it *exactly*, I've only just had the idea.'

'I should *probably* add that I don't have

any time-travel spells at the moment,' said Lily. '*Sorry!*'

'All right . . . It was only an *idea*,' muttered Jack.

'Just not a very good one,' said Red, who was feeling a bit tired and cross.

'It's better than anything *you've* come up with so far!' replied Jack.

'Oh *yeah*?!' yelled Red, her eyes narrowing. 'What about the plan where we all dressed up like Big Bad Wolves and attacked Fitch's palace?'

'That was *stupid*!' protested Jack. 'Anansi's the tallest and he's only four feet tall! We'd look like Small Silly Wolves!'

'Fine!' shouted Red angrily.

'*Fine!*' repeated Jack, but a little bit louder.

'OK, *OK*! This isn't getting us anywhere!' interrupted Lily. 'Let's take a break and go and check on the cutting from the Story Tree. I mean, that's why you came down here, right? To check that it's still growing? Come on, it's just this way . . .'

They swam through to another section of the cave where a small tree grew in a bubble that floated in the middle of a bright shaft of sunlight.

'Whoa!' exclaimed Red and Jack, forgetting all about their argument.

'It's grown *really* big!' said Red. 'Just as well! If Mayor Fitch carries on the way he has been, *nobody's* going to be able to use the *real* Story Tree. Just think! All those stories – they'll be lost forever if Fitch gets his way!' She shook her head sadly. 'And *this* cutting will be all that's left of it.'

'Still, it *is* doing pretty well,' replied Lily, looking at the small tree. 'That nature wizard guy has been popping in every now and then to check on it – like *he* knows anything about *anything*!'

'The Green Man?' asked Jack, looking confused. 'But doesn't he know *everything* about plants and trees and, well, anything that grows?'

'Yeah, I suppose so,' said Lily with

a scowl. 'It's just that I offered to cast a spell to make it rainbow-coloured, or pink and fluffy, or *something*. You know, brighten it up a bit! But he said the best way for me to help was to *never* touch it, not to go near it and to try not to even *look* at it. I mean, I thought that was kind of rude, but I guess some people just like plain old *boring* trees.'

Red's eyes shot open. 'Some people like trees . . .' she said slowly, as though it was really important.

'Er, yeah,' said Lily. 'Boring old ordinary ones—'

'Some people like trees . . .'

interrupted Red, smiling slowly. She looked round at everyone as though they should know what on earth she was thinking.

'Wha Aaa Aaaa t?' muttered Betsy.

'Yeah . . . I think the shock of everything must have got to her,' replied Jack, looking concerned.

'You don't understand!' exclaimed Red excitedly. '*Some people like trees. Like Wilf!* The huntsman who always wanted to be a woodsman – *remember?*' She looked over at Jack.

'Yeah, he helped us rescue Anansi's mum from that

witch, before she got . . . you know, captured again.'

'That's *right*! And what else does Wilf have?' she asked. Jack looked blankly at her and shrugged,

'A slightly strange haircut?'

'No!' said Red, looking annoyed. 'Well . . . yes, *slightly* . . . but what else?'

'WhaAaaaat!' squawked Betsy excitedly.

'*Exactly!*' Red was now grinning wildly. 'He's got a pet dragon!'

3

Rescue

ed, Jack and Betsy left Lily's cave and crept back through Tale Town to the hideout in the woods where their friends were waiting for them, along with Professor Hendricks and the rest of the gorillas.

Jack and Red were telling everyone about what had happened with Wolfie, as well as their genius idea of getting Wilf to help – but nobody else seemed very convinced.

'So, let me get this straight . . .' said Anansi, frowning. 'Wolfie's been captured? And all Hurrilan's trolls are going to attack Tale Town?'

Jack nodded.

Anansi frowned even more. 'And while you, Hansel, Gretel, Ella, Cole and Betsy are going to rescue Wolfie . . . me, Rapunzel and Red are *somehow* going to stop a whole troll army?'

'Yes!' said Red encouragingly. 'Along with Wilf.'

'The *ex*-huntsman,' said Anansi, not sounding impressed.

'*And* his dragon!' added Jack enthusiastically, sensing that none of this was going down particularly well.

'Ah yes, I'd forgotten about the blind dragon for a minute,' said Anansi.

'She's *partially sighted*,' corrected Red. 'Anyway, a dragon's a dragon. I remember you were pretty terrified the first time you met her.'

'Yeah, but I'm *me*!' protested Anansi as he sat back in one of the rickety wooden chairs. 'We're talking about fighting off an army of trolls here!'

Hansel, Gretel, Cole, Ella, Rapunzel and Anansi looked doubtfully round at each other.

'So, how *exactly* is it going to work?' asked Ella. 'I mean, we've got the dragon, but what else?'

'Erm . . .' said Red, who hadn't really thought about anything beyond *having a dragon.*

'Ahh . . .' said Jack slowly,

trying to think
of *something* sensible to say.

Then Betsy squawked
'WHAAAAT!' very loudly.

'*Exactly!*' said Jack. 'What
we *also* have is a plan!' He
looked relieved and quietly
whispered, '*Thanks, Betsy!*'

'Oh goody,' said
Rapunzel sarcastically. 'For
a minute there I thought it

was all *completely* hopeless.'

Jack glared at Rapunzel and continued: 'Look, the trolls will be marching down from the north. *Right?*'

Everyone nodded and peered down as Jack picked up a stick and scratched out a simple map on the floor. 'So they'll *have* to come over the bridge at Quidgely's Pass — it's the only way down from the north. *Right?*' Again, everyone nodded.

'So . . . what if there's no bridge?' finished Jack, waving his stick with a flourish. 'Together with Wilf and his dragon, you can burn down the bridge and *then* the trolls won't be able to get here. At least, not without going a *really* long way around — which will take ages!'

'You know, that *might* actually work,' said Anansi excitedly. 'We'll have to move quickly though if they're coming at dawn.'

Professor Hendricks leaned forward to take the stick from Jack and began scratching words out on the ground.

This was how the gorillas communicated. They were all incredibly clever, but couldn't actually *speak*. Everyone looked down eagerly to see what words of wisdom the professor was writing.

'I'M A BIT PECKISH. DOES ANYONE KNOW IF THERE ARE ANY OF THOSE LOVELY COCONUT BISCUITS LEFT?'

As well as being clever, the gorillas were nearly always hungry.

'In the storage cupboard,' said Rapunzel briskly.

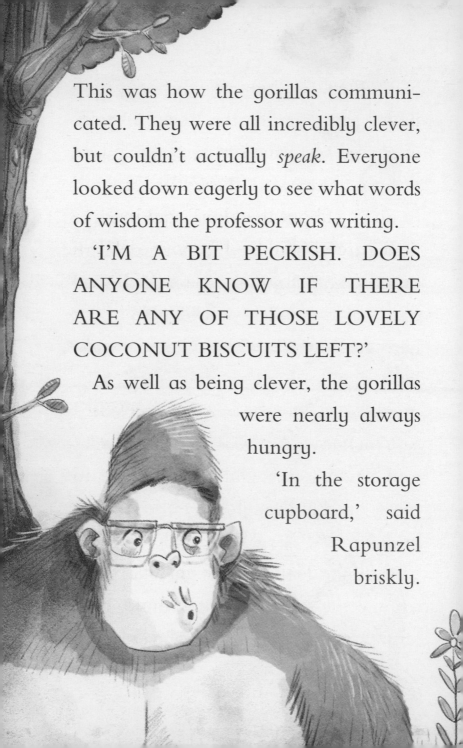

'Top shelf, on the right.' She tutted under her breath as the professor lumbered off. '*Honestly*, why doesn't he just go and look for himself?'

'So . . . about the plan?' said Jack.

'It's great!' said Red, beaming. 'We'll go and stop the trolls with Wilf and then you guys can rescue Wolfie!'

'Well that all sounds OK –' began Hansel.

'– but how are we going to find Wilf?' finished Gretel.

'The spells we got from Lily,' said Jack, brandishing a blue glass bottle. 'We've got a "spell of summoning" here!'

'Cool!' whispered Ella.

'*And* a "spell of shocking"!'

'*Ooooh!*' exclaimed Anansi.

'*And* a "spell of spelling"!'

'How's *that* going to help us here?' interrupted Rapunzel.

'Well, perhaps it won't,' said Jack defensively, 'but I've always found spelling some words a bit difficult. Anyway, there's also a "spell of scattering", "scorching", "searching", "sheltering", "smashing" *and* "skill".' He paused, and then added, 'Lily could only find the key to the "*Spells beginning with S*" cupboard.'

'Brilliant!' said Red. 'With all that, *and* the five of you, Mayor Fitch's guards don't stand a chance. Wolfie's going to be back with us in no time! Let's summon Wilf and his dragon and get going!'

<hr />

'Arghhhhhh!' yelled Jack as he sprinted down the corridors of Mayor Fitch's palace. Hansel was just behind him, and zipping through the air alongside was Ella's Fairy Godbrother, Cole. They were *also* both screaming. Betsy was flapping along too, as fast as she could.

This probably seems like a bad way to try to sneak in somewhere to rescue your friend, but they'd already done the sneaking-around bit and it hadn't really worked out.

It all started well enough when Jack had planted one of his magic beanstalks outside Fitch's palace,* and then Ella, Hansel, Gretel, Cole, Jack and Betsy had all crept in through an open window on the fourth floor.

They'd used the 'spell of sheltering' to be able to move around the castle without being seen and everything had *seemed* to be working . . . at first. Using the 'spell of searching' they easily found their way to the dungeons where Wolfie was being held. They called out to Wolfie through the door but he just lay there curled up on his bed, covered in blankets and whimpering. Ella rummaged around in her tangled hair,

* The palace *actually* belonged to Rapunzel's parents, the king and queen, but since he'd banished them, Fitch had decided that perhaps he should move in there instead.

pulled out a lock-picking kit and got to work. A few seconds later the door swung open as Ella and Gretel crept into the cell, but as they pulled back the blankets, they saw that Wolfie had a blindfold covering his eyes and ears.

Suddenly one of Fitch's guards burst out from behind a hidden door, grabbed

Wolfie, Gretel *and* Ella, then dragged them all away, before slamming the cell door, leaving Hansel, Jack, Cole and Betsy outside.

'Quick!' shouted Hansel. 'Use the "spell of smashing" to break down the door!'

Jack pulled out a glass vial and drank it in one swig.

'*Dodecahedron*!' he shouted dramatically.

'Is that part of the spell?' said Cole, looking around anxiously. 'Nothing's happening yet!'

'A three-dimensional shape with twelve sides,' said Jack, looking confused, and then spelled out D, O, D, E, C, A, H, E, D, R, O, N slowly and clearly.

'Wrong spell!' groaned Hansel.

'That was the "*spelling* spell"!' added Cole.

'I knew I should have labelled them!' muttered Jack, pulling out another bottle.

'Wait a minute . . .' said Hansel. 'Let's just try opening it first.' He stepped forward and pushed at the main jail door, which swung slowly, creakily open. Hansel grinned at Jack as they crept into the cell and then tried the hidden door inside there. That *also* opened and Jack was just about to say, 'Well, this is going to be *easy*!' when four of the largest, most ferocious guard dogs he had *ever* seen burst out. So he didn't say that. He just screamed and ran away as fast as he could.

'Arghhhhhh!' yelled Jack as he sprinted down the corridors of Mayor Fitch's palace, followed by Hansel, Betsy and Cole. In a blind panic Jack pulled out a spell at random. It was the spell of scattering'; perhaps *that* would make the pack of dogs break up? He drank the whole bottle and there was an intense flare of light and smoke. As it cleared, Jack could still hear the snarling dogs just behind him, but none of his friends. It was *them* who had been scattered.

'These spells could really do with some sort of instructions,' he thought as he ran on alone. He pulled out *another* bottle – the 'spell of scorching' – and eyed it warily. *Hopefully* it would scorch the dogs, or the floor, so that they couldn't run on it. But what if it *didn't* work like that? By now the dogs were right behind him, so he decided to just go for it. The magic tasted smoky and hot, rasping on his tongue as it slipped down his throat.

'GAhhhhhhHHHHhh!' yelled Jack, feeling incredibly hot as all his clothes started smouldering.

'Seriously?' he thought. Why would

anyone want a spell that made *them* scorched?

As Jack sprinted down the corridor he left thick trails of smoke behind him, which at least distracted the dogs for a moment.

But only for a moment . . .

Soon they were back after him. Their teeth snapped at his ankles and spittle swung around their slathering jaws. Jack's heart was thumping and his legs were aching – he was a fast runner, but the dogs showed no sign of stopping, or even slowing. There was no choice but to try the 'spell of smashing' and just hope that it wasn't going to smash *him*. Nervously he took the bottle out, yanked off the top and drank it. Suddenly he felt *incredibly* strong. His muscles seemed to be working by themselves as he ran. Cracks appeared on the stone slabs as his feet struck the ground. *This* was more like it! He carried on, his feet pounding harder and harder. Clouds of dust and broken shards of rock started flying out from beneath him. The loud crashing noise made the dogs nervous and they slowed down as Jack ran on, his feet hammering like pistons until, all of a sudden, the ground behind him gave way and tumbled down, leaving a wide gap that even the most crazed of devil dogs wouldn't try to jump over.

Furiously the dogs skidded to a halt and howled at Jack, who turned for a moment and laughed at them.

He'd made it! He was going to get out!

Then his heart sank. *Maybe . . .* but he was also *completely* alone. What had happened to his friends?

4

Take Me to the Bridge!

The sun was starting to rise as Anansi swung under the bridge that spanned Quidgely's Pass on a long thread of spider silk. Anansi had the power to speak with spiders and ask them for help whenever he needed it. Like when he needed some spider silk to swing from, or if he found a jar that he just *couldn't* open – spiders are surprisingly good at that sort of thing.

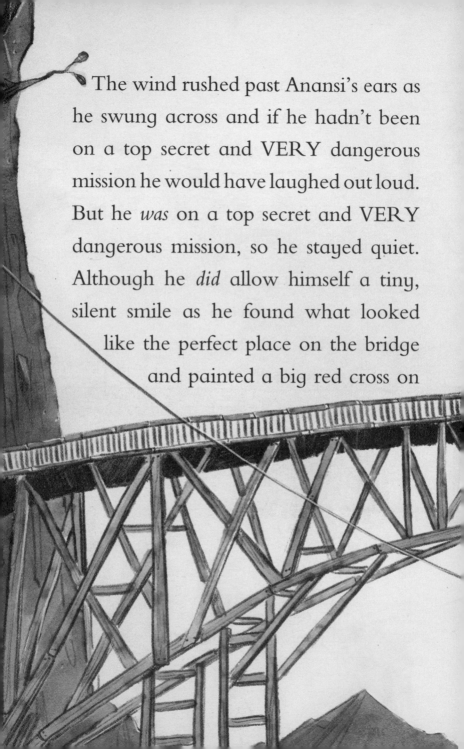

The wind rushed past Anansi's ears as he swung across and if he hadn't been on a top secret and VERY dangerous mission he would have laughed out loud. But he *was* on a top secret and VERY dangerous mission, so he stayed quiet. Although he *did* allow himself a tiny, silent smile as he found what looked like the perfect place on the bridge and painted a big red cross on

the wooden struts. Then he swung
back towards Wilf, Red and Rapunzel.

After they'd used the spell of
summoning to call Wilf it had taken
no time at all to convince him to help,
and not much longer for his dragon,
Destiny, to fly them to Quidgely's Pass.

'*Nearly there now, Missy!*' Wilf
bellowed, even though

Red had told him at least fifteen times that they were outlaws and this was a *very* secret mission. The trouble with Wilf was that he seemed to be incapable of using anything less than his outdoors voice. Actually, it was more like his cheering-on-the-local-football-team-when-they've-just-scored voice. Still, they needed his help, so they just tried to get him to say as little as possible.

Red had hit upon the idea of asking Wilf's dragon, Destiny, to burn down the bridge so the trolls wouldn't be able to get across the ravine and attack Tale Town. That would be *it* – problem solved!

Rapunzel had seemed a bit uneasy at the thought of burning down the *only* bridge leading to Tale Town from the north, as it seemed a teeny bit, well . . . *naughty*. But Red and Anansi had insisted that it was the *only* thing they could do: otherwise there would be a full-scale troll army attacking Tale Town. And wasn't one burned-down bridge a bit *less bad* than a war?

Rapunzel had supposed that *perhaps* it was . . .

When they landed near the bridge to take a closer look, Wilf explained that Destiny *actually* had a bit of a sore throat so they'd need to find some hot honey and lemon for her — as well as *ideally* a few hundred cough sweets too. Also, it would be

good if they could find the best spot for her to aim at on the bridge and paint a target for her. Preferably something simple, like a big red cross. After all, her eyesight *wasn't* what it used to be.

So that was why Anansi was swinging along under the bridge while Rapunzel and Red went running through the nearby woods trying to 'borrow' as much honeycomb as they could from some *very* irritable bees. Every time they went back to Wilf he sent them out for more, saying things like, 'Destiny's a dragon, not a guinea pig! We need a *lot* more lemons than that!' or 'Any luck with the cough sweets yet?'

'No, Wilf,' said Rapunzel flatly. 'We're in the middle of a wood. *Remember?* We're lucky enough to find *lemons* growing here. I don't think there're going to be any *cough-sweet trees* nearby. Do you?'

'Hmm, that *is* a shame!' said Wilf, looking anxiously at Destiny and the tin bath full of honey and lemon heating up over a campfire.

'See, without the cough sweets I'm not sure we'll get the old girl's fire-breath back!'

'You really could have mentioned that *before* we agreed the plan!' muttered Rapunzel under her breath.

Red had just come back from her most recent trip into the woods with thirty-eight lemons, twelve large chunks of honeycomb and three bee stings when an arrow whistled through the air towards them. They looked over to the far side of Quidgely's Pass as the first lookout of a huge troll army approached. They didn't seem to be in a very friendly mood.

'*Quick!*' shouted Rapunzel. 'We need to do this *now!*'

Destiny ducked her head down towards the tin bath full of honey and lemon and drank the whole lot in one go. Then she sprang into the air on her huge muscular legs and banked sharply round so that she was facing the bridge. Wilf steered her towards the cross that Anansi had painted and as they got closer he shouted, '*Fire it up!*' and patted the dragon on the side of her neck.

Destiny took a deep breath, opened her mouth as wide as she could and then out burst . . . *nothing*.

'Er, now would be a good time for the fire!' yelped Anansi as an arrow shot past, just missing him.

'Give her a chance!' said Wilf. 'Destiny don't like to feel under pressure.'

'I'm sure she doesn't!' said Rapunzel. 'But if she doesn't breathe fire soon then we're all going to be feeling under pressure, *and* spears, arrows and lots of other sharp things — *look*!'

She pointed up at the troll army who were approaching the edge of the ravine and aiming weapons down towards them.

Destiny banked round and soared high into the sky, preparing for another run. As she did so, an arrow shot upward, tearing through the thin membrane of her right wing. She faltered for a moment, then swept down so that she was flying alongside the bridge. Arrows, rocks and all sorts of hard, sharp and unwanted things flew down towards them, but Destiny curled, weaved and dodged round all of them, opening her

mouth wide and breathing in before *finally* sending out a huge torrent of burning flame that struck Anansi's target. The flames took immediately and it wasn't long before the whole bridge was alight. Destiny flew back and they landed on their side of the pass – safely out of range of the trolls' angry shouts and, more importantly, their weapons.

'*Yes!*' shouted Anansi, punching the air. 'We did it!' He looked around at his friends, and saw Red and Rapunzel smiling, their faces reflecting the warm red glow of the flames. Wilf was bending over Destiny's wing, inspecting it. The tear from the arrow had grown bigger and ran almost to the tip.

'You all right, my darlin'?' Wilf asked the dragon, who looked over and nodded.

'You're a brave one, and no mistake!' he said, ruffling the scales on the back of her neck. 'All the same, you ain't flying *anywhere* until we get that looked at. You hear me?'

The dragon nodded glumly.

'Sorry, folks,' said Wilf. 'Looks like you'll be walkin' home. I need to get the old girl fixed up.'

'But . . . she'll be *OK*, won't she?' asked Red, stroking Destiny's snout.

'Oh, aye! She'll be fine. She's seen worse!' The dragon nodded again, looking braver as Red gave Wilf a big hug.

'Thanks for your help,' she said. 'I *knew* we could count on you!'

'Well, what can I say? It was my Destiny, really!' Wilf waved goodbye to Red and her friends, and then turned to lead the dragon into the shelter of the woods.

Red's mirror pinged and she flipped it open to see Quartz's face looking back at her.

'I think that worked!' he whispered. 'I don't know for certain, but everyone *definitely* seems *very* annoyed! Well done!'

Then his image faded away and the mirror showed Red's reflection again.

'Right then!' said Rapunzel. 'Let's get back to the hideout. I can't *wait* to see the look on their faces when we tell them we stopped an entire troll army!'

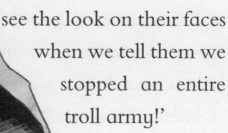

5

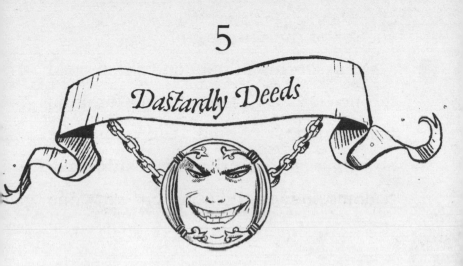

Dastardly Deeds

Mayor Fitch sat on a big, gold throne, in a big, gold room, holding a big, gold picture of himself, painted in gold. He nodded approvingly: it was a good painting. He was about to pass it over to a member of his private guard to hang on the gold wall when he paused. Perhaps he could encourage *everyone* to have one of these paintings in their homes, to remind them of all he had done for them?

Fitch sat happily back in his gold throne. Sure, it was a bit uncomfortable, but it *was* made of gold! If you wanted a normal *comfy* chair then you could have one, just like all the other peasants. He

shuddered slightly as he thought about the *ordinary* people. To think that for all these years everyone had just been using the Story Tree whenever they felt like it – Tale Town's most precious gift given away to any old fool, for *free*! It was shocking! He smiled as he thought about his secret plan to stop everyone else but him using the Story Tree. And if the people of Tale Town didn't like it – he'd banish them.

'Mayor Fitch, sir?' called a voice, cutting through his thoughts.

'Mmmm?'

'We have news on the wall, sir.'

'And?'

'It's *er*, ready, sir. It's not quite fully built yet, but all the machinery inside is working perfectly. We just tested it on one of the troll prisoners and now *he's* powerless and *we* can use all his magic!'

'Well, that's just marvellous!' purred Fitch, rubbing his podgy fingers together. 'When those ghastly green beasts escaped from their Secret Mountain I felt . . .'

'Er, some of the trolls are blue, sir,' said the guard. Fitch said nothing and glared at him. The guard looked a bit uneasy but carried on talking. 'Yes, that's right, sir. Blue, sir. And some of them are purple too. It's only actually the earth trolls that are green, and even then, a lot of them are a sort of grey colour. In fact, it's quite fascinating . . .'

'*Guards!*' yelled Fitch as the man in front of him looked up, surprised. 'Arrest this man. He's a traitor and is to be banished.'

'*Banished*, sir?' asked one of the other guards who had just run in.

'Yes! *Banished!*' barked Fitch. 'You know, made to leave!'

'Well, I know what "banished" means, sir, it's just that . . .

well, that's *Frank*. He's been your most loyal guard for fifteen years.'

'I'm aware of who he is,' said Fitch, glaring unpleasantly down at the guard who had just spoken. 'Just do it!' He paused and then said, 'Actually, one more thing. When you've banished him . . .'

'Yes, sir?'

'Then banish yourself!' Fitch smiled triumphantly. 'Now, off you trot, both of you!' He circled his fingers to call over a couple of his especially unpleasant bodyguards and smiled as the two confused new traitors were dragged backwards out of the throne room.

'Right,' he said, clapping his hands

together lightly. 'On to the trolls! The wall is in place, so I propose we get started. I think we need a real test of our new equipment. Hefferson!'

'Sir?' replied one of the guards.

'I want you to go and break a hole in the Moonstone defences.'

'*What?* But, sir, that's the only thing that keeps the trolls out!'

Fitch glared at him, 'Yes, I know. *And?*'

'Well, if we do *that*, then won't the trolls get in?'

'*Precisely!*' exclaimed Fitch. 'The trolls will think it's the perfect opportunity to attack! And when they do . . . *we'll* be waiting for them! Using the new machinery in the walls we'll be able to drain every last drop of magic from every last troll, and then *finally*, we'll be rid of them – *forever*!

6

Cold Spaghetti

*J*ack trudged wearily through the woods. The mission had been a complete failure. They'd gone to rescue Wolfie, but in the end he'd lost *everyone*. Jack had hidden away in a high tree with a clear view of the palace and waited for more than an hour, but *none* of his friends had made it out. He then looked around the town, down on the beach and went searching deep within the Wild Woods.

But he saw no one. In the end, with nothing left to do, and nowhere else to go, he went back to the hideout.

He made the secret wolf howl as he approached, but there was no response. The hideout was deserted. Not even Professor Hendricks or the other gorillas were there. This was very odd . . . Looking around for clues, Jack eventually found a trail of banana skins that led through the trees, where there were

ARROOOOOo.!

signs of a scuffle next to heavy cart tracks leading back towards Tale Town. Had their hideout been discovered? It certainly looked like it, and now the gorillas had been captured *too*!

Was it really just *him* left? What could he *possibly* do on his own? Jack sank to the floor, suddenly feeling very lonely.

'There, there! Come on now, don't cry,' said a small bowl of spaghetti as it hopped across the floor.

'Yiiiiiiiiiikes!' yelped Jack, scrambling away.

'It'll be OK,' said the bowl of spaghetti soothingly, as a few strands flopped out and made a clumsy attempt at patting him on the back.

'Er . . .' mumbled Jack, backing away.

'Oh yes, I'd better explain . . .' said the bowl of spaghetti. 'It's me, *Cole*! I had a bit of a, well, a bit of a mix-up at the palace. I tried to cast a spell to make me *faster*, but I must have said it wrong as it made me *pasta* instead.' The bowl of spaghetti somehow managed to look annoyed. 'Why is doing magic so tricksy? You have to get every little detail JUST right!'

'I see . . .' said Jack slowly. Everybody knew that Cole's magic was a bit *unpredictable* – nearly every spell he ever cast went wrong – but *this* was a particularly impressive mess-up, even by Cole's standards.

'It worked, though!' said Cole proudly. 'None of the guards was looking for a bowl of cold spaghetti.'

'I suppose not,' said Jack doubtfully. 'Any idea how long you'll be like that?'

'Possibly forever.' The bowl sniffed loudly. 'I'm a *rubbish* Fairy Godbrother!'

'Hey, no you're not!' said Jack, trying to cheer Cole up.

'I *am*,' wailed Cole. 'I saw all the others get captured and dragged off to the palace dungeons and I couldn't do *anything* to stop it, because . . . well . . .' The strands of spaghetti flopped around sadly.

'It's not your fault!' insisted Jack. 'You tried your best!'

'Yeah? Well, I guess it wasn't good enough,' replied Cole miserably.

'Now Ella's been captured, along with everyone else, and no offence, Jack, but what are we going to do about that? I mean, you don't have any special skills like Anansi or Rapunzel, and *I'm* a bowl of cold spaghetti.'

'Wait!' cried Jack. 'Maybe I don't . . . *yet*!' He rooted around in his satchel and pulled out the last two spells he'd been given by Lily: the 'spell of shocking' and the 'spell of skill'. 'If we share this "skill" potion, then *you'll* be able to turn yourself back to normal, and *I'll* be able to . . . Well, I don't know what I'll be able to do, but I *bet* it'll be cool!' He pulled the stopper out, drank half of the potion and poured the other half over the spaghetti.

There was a bright flash and a ring of bright blue smoke shot out from where the bowl had been.

'*Wow!*' said Cole, who was back to normal and hovering in the air. 'That was *easy*! I feel like I could do, well . . . *anything*!'

———— ◆ ————

A few minutes later, after Jack had discovered that he could suddenly speak twelve different languages (including 'dog') and perform amazing kung fu skills, and Cole had walked a tightrope blindfolded while playing the guitar, they decided that they should probably stop messing about and start working out how to rescue their friends.

'How long do you think this will

last?' asked Cole, making an earwig twenty times bigger, then quickly putting it back to its normal size when he realized that giant earwigs were *actually* quite scary. 'I hope it's ages!'

'*I know!*' said Jack. 'Being really good at things is *awesome*! And now that I'm amazing at planning, I've worked out that even *with* our new skills, we're *still* going to need help because we don't know how long the spell will last.'

'But who can help us?' asked Cole.

'All our friends have been kidnapped.'

'Yes,' agreed Jack with a smile. 'All our *friends* have been . . .'

'What do you mean?' asked Cole.

'Well, he's not exactly a friend, and I know that Red won't like this . . . but I know one person who'd do *anything* to get Wolfie back safely.'

'And who's that?'

'His dad,' said Jack. 'The Big Bad Wolf!'

7

The Big Bad Wolf

*H*aving a huge wolf burst out of the woods, snarling something about licking your gizzards off a stick like a lollipop, is alarming, even if you don't know *exactly* what 'gizzards' are – which Jack didn't. Still, when you're amazingly skilled at pretty much everything in the world, things like that are less of a problem. Jack had discovered he was *also* an expert wolf

whisperer. He'd marched right up to the Big Bad Wolf and gently blown down his nose while stroking underneath his chin. Within seconds Jack had managed to calm the Big Bad Wolf down, *and* got him to agree to help them save Wolfie – although he did have to tickle him behind the ears to do that bit.

'So, where's this Fitch fella got my boy?' demanded the Big Bad Wolf.

'Er, he's in the palace dungeons in Tale Town, Mr Wolf,' replied Jack, 'along with all our other friends. They got captured during our last rescue attempt.'

'Typical humans!' muttered the Big Bad Wolf under his breath. 'Ain't no good for nothin'. It's about time it was us wolves callin' the shots!'

'Sorry, what was that, Mr Wolf?' said Jack.

'I just said it was about time!'

'*What's* the time, Mr Wolf?' asked Jack, feeling confused.

'Oh, never mind,' said the Big Bad Wolf. '*So* . . . how are we doin' this? Is it just you, me and that little blue ghost thing?'

Cole looked deeply offended, but didn't quite dare to actually say anything – the Big Bad Wolf really was *very* scary.

'Look, we've got

skills!' said Jack, hopping into a one-fingered handstand and making a cat's cradle with his feet. 'Right now, Cole and I can do pretty much *anything*, so with your help, we'll get Wolfie back in no time! But we need to hurry. I'm not sure how long the spell's going to last.'

The Big Bad Wolf shrugged. 'Fair enough,' he said. 'If it involves terrorizing Tale Town then I'm in.'

There was a rustle in the bushes behind them. Jack looked urgently over at Cole, who quickly made them all invisible. They waited as the rustling got louder. Soon they could hear quiet, murmured voices. Jack watched as the Big Bad Wolf crouched down, preparing to pounce. The wolf's eyes narrowed and he licked his lips hungrily.

Some leaves next to Jack were swept aside and then a small group walked into the clearing. The wolf roared and leaped out, his claws flashing in the dim light as three terrified figures screamed and jumped backwards.

It was Red, Rapunzel and Anansi.

8

Rescue: Take Two

It was safe to say that the reunion between Red and the Big Bad Wolf was *not* going particularly well.

'I cannot *believe* that you ATE my *grandmother!*' shouted Red angrily.

'I thought she was a deer,' protested the Big Bad Wolf, not entirely convincingly.

'Walking on *two legs?*' spat Red.

'She had a walking stick,' protested

the wolf, 'so technically it was three. Anyway, it was misty, I couldn't see very well.'

'But you followed her into her house!'

'Deer are *very* good at hiding.'

'. . . And you ate her!'

'Yeah, well . . .'

'And *then* you dressed up as *her* and tried to eat ME!'

'The thing is . . .' The wolf paused again, unable to come up with a good explanation. 'Look.' He sighed. 'I'm sorry. If it makes you feel any better, she tasted horrible and, besides, your dad *did* manage to get her back, so no harm done . . .' He unconsciously ran a paw over the long scar that ran along his middle.

'*Sorry* . . . Can I interrupt?' asked Jack. 'It's just that we've got to go and rescue everyone before Cole goes back to being rubbish at magic – no offence, Cole. So can we *please* just get on with the rescue, and then you two can carry on fighting afterwards? OK?'

Red glared at him, then muttered, 'OK.'

The Big Bad Wolf growled low in his throat and made the tiniest of nods.

'Good,' said Jack. '*Thank you*. OK, Cole, can you teleport us inside the palace?'

'I can do better than *that*!' Cole grinned and clicked his fingers. 'I can teleport us right inside Wolfie's cell!'

———◆———

In the woods to the north of Tale Town something was happening. As the sun was setting over the treetops, shadowy figures were walking along the many twisting pathways. They moved silently towards a large clearing where several hundred other figures were already gathered. It was a mixed group. There were trolls, there were imps, there were sprites, there were the tiny, inch-high people of Tom Thumb's village, along with four giants, three minotaurs, two centaurs and one Humpty Dumpty. Together they were

planning their revenge. Over the years, Mayor Fitch had been sending out his guards to raid, steal, plunder and take whatever he wanted from *all* of them. Individually, they hadn't been able to do anything to stop Fitch – but together? *Together*, they stood a chance.

The troll leader Hurrilan looked out at his ever-growing army. It hadn't taken them long to find a way to cross Quidgely's Pass. When you can control stone, to make it do whatever you like, a broken bridge isn't really a problem.

Soon they would be able to strike. Soon it would *all* be over!

───────── ◆ ─────────

With a bright blue flash, Red, Rapunzel, Jack, Anansi, Cole and the Big Bad Wolf appeared in Wolfie's cell, but he wasn't alone. Betsy and Ella had also been locked up in the same room.

'WhaAaaAaaaaat?!' yelped Betsy, Ella and Wolfie in surprise, which made the guards unlock the door and burst in to find out what was going on.

They were angry at first, but that anger soon became fear as the Big Bad Wolf prowled towards them.

'Now . . . you been keepin' my boy 'ere against his will!' snarled the wolf. 'So I'm going to give you a simple choice. You can either run out of here screaming, "Help me, Mummy!" and leave them doors wide open. Or . . .' He looked at them closely so they could see themselves reflected in the dark pools of his eyes. 'Or I can eat you up whole. It's your choice. I'm happy either way.'

Before he'd even finished there was the loud clanging of a door as three guards ran out screaming, 'Help me, Mummy!'

'Well, that's a shame!' muttered the

Big Bad Wolf. 'I was a bit hungry.'

'*Dad!*' cried Wolfie, running up and throwing his arms around him. 'You came for me! And you're with . . . *my friends!*'

The Big Bad Wolf brushed something that looked suspiciously like a tear from his furry face. 'Yeah, well, couldn't have you all cooped up now, could I? I mean, there ain't even any shampoo in 'ere!'

'And you don't mind that I'm friends with . . . well . . . with the humans?'

The Big Bad Wolf ruffled his son's fur. 'Listen . . . You and me might not be cut from the same cloth. We might not do things the same way. But you know what?' Wolfie looked up at his dad, who smiled. 'You're my *son*. And more than that, I'm proud of you! Not even your great-great-grandad, Heartslash Sharpclaw, would have gone up against Fitch like you kids have. Now, don't you have some other friends that need rescuing? We're two short, ain't we?'

'WhaAaa Aaaaat!' squawked Betsy urgently.

'*What?*' said the Big Bad Wolf. 'What do you mean, "*What!*"?'

'WhaAaa Aaaaat!' repeated Betsy

angrily, flapping her wings for added emphasis.

'She said that Hansel and Gretel are in the cells on the next floor down,' explained Jack. 'Apparently, they were being a bit naughty and had to get locked up away from everyone else.'

'Yes!' added Ella. 'They also had to write out "I must not knock off the guards' helmets with a stone, steal the keys and then try to escape" one hundred times each!'

The magic mirror in Red's pocket pinged and everyone fell silent as she opened it up. There was Quartz's face, and in the background was what looked like Greentop's Cafe.

'Er, hi,' whispered Quartz.

'So . . . I've got some good news and some bad news.'

'What's the bad news?' asked Red.

'We got over Quidgely's Pass and the whole troll army is waiting just outside Tale Town. We're resting in the woods

to have something to eat before the big attack.'

'OK . . .' said Red, looking worried. 'So, what's the *good* news? You've got a plan that means we'll be able to defeat Mayor Fitch *and* stop Hurrilan from attacking and ruining the already *terrible* relations between the trolls and the humans?'

'Er, no, *sorry*. The good news is that this cafe makes *delicious* milkshakes.'

'Right,' said Red. 'So . . . not really *great* news, is it?'

'No, I guess not . . .'

'OK. Look, thanks for the warning, but I'm a bit busy trying to escape from a dungeon right now, so can we, like, chat later?'

'Yeah. Sure. Good luck!' replied Quartz, and his reflection in the mirror faded away.

'So, you all heard that?' asked Red, looking round at her friends. They all nodded.

'And does anyone have any brainwaves about how to fix this mess?'

They all shook their heads and Red sighed.

'I think that's a *no*,' replied Ella. 'Still, on the bright side, at least the cell door's open!'

'I suppose . . .' muttered Red.

'We'll have to be careful, though,' added Ella. 'There are *loads* of Fitch's men in the palace and they're *really* mean!'

Jack picked up a sword that one of the guards had dropped, and twirled it around through the air in an amazingly complex series of movements. 'I don't think we need to worry too much about *that*,' he said with a smile. 'Not while we've got our skills! Right, Cole?'

'*Right*,' agreed Cole as he clicked his fingers and made a large pile of ice

cream appear in a messy heap on top of the Big Bad Wolf.

'*Wait* . . . Sorry! That wasn't what I meant to . . .' He ducked suddenly as the sword Jack had been spinning flew out of his fingers, shot through the air and clanged against the wall before falling to the floor.

'Oh,' said Cole sadly. 'Looks like the spell's finished.'

9

Hubert Helps

*O*nce Cole's magic was back to normal (meaning that it didn't work) and Jack's only *real* skill was that he could wiggle each ear one at a time, things were not looking *quite* so good. The car trick was definitely a good one, but even so, it wasn't going to stop a prison full of armed guards.

'I'll call some spiders,' whispered Anansi, making a soft clicking noise in the back of his throat. Soon the floor was carpeted with thousands of spiders, all looking up at Anansi.

'*Hubert!*' said Anansi to one small spider that was crawling up his arm. 'How's it going? I've not seen you for *ages*! How's your mum – did she get that leg fixed up?' The spider rubbed its mandibles together and Anansi smiled. 'Oh, *good*! Well, you tell her to be more careful next time. Anyway, I need to ask you guys a little favour . . .'

Five minutes later there was a tunnel made of spider webs running all the way down the corridor. The web tunnel clung to the shadowy corners of the ceiling leading towards the staircase that led down to where Hansel and Gretel were imprisoned. One by one, they climbed up into the tunnel. Jack had just helped to heave Ella up when the guards came running back, along with dozens of reinforcements.

Red, Jack and their friends crept slowly along the woven webs. They had *nearly* made it to the staircase when one of the guards happened to look up and notice them.

'There!' she shouted. 'They're hiding up there!'

All the guards craned their necks to look up.

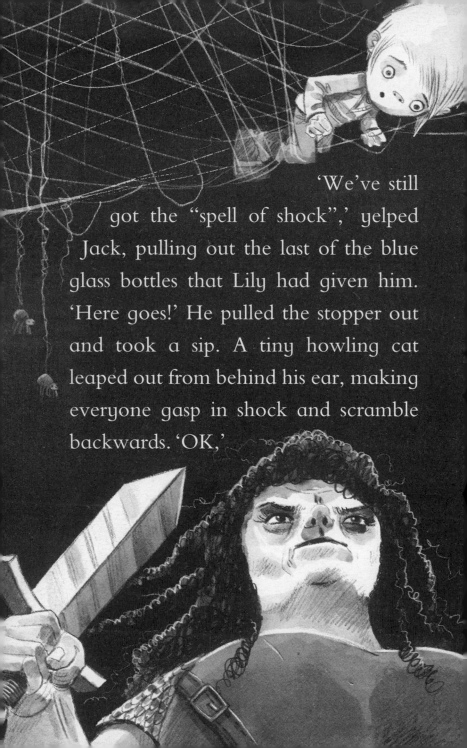

'We've still got the "spell of shock",' yelped Jack, pulling out the last of the blue glass bottles that Lily had given him. 'Here goes!' He pulled the stopper out and took a sip. A tiny howling cat leaped out from behind his ear, making everyone gasp in shock and scramble backwards. 'OK,'

he muttered. 'Not *exactly* what I was imagining . . .'

'Perhaps you just need more?' suggested Ella. So Jack tipped his head back and drank the whole spell. Soon the corridor was overrun with howling, shrieking, hissing cats. They leaped out of the guards' trousers, from behind flickering torches, out of tiny air vents and anywhere that you wouldn't expect a cat to leap out from.

'*Now!*' yelled Red as a cat sprang out of her hood. '*Run!* While they're all distracted!'

As the guards scrambled around in a sea of black cats, the

children leaped out of the web and darted down the spiral staircase to the level below. At the end of the corridor they could see Hansel and Gretel peering out towards them.

'There they are!' cried Rapunzel. 'We've got to hurry – the guards will be down here any second!'

'Yes!' exclaimed a voice from behind them. '*Yes*. They will.' Coming down the

staircase was Mayor Fitch, surrounded by his personal bodyguards and more soldiers than you could even count.

Wolfie's dad turned and flung himself at the soldiers, his teeth and claws flashing, but although he was able to hold the guards back, there was *nowhere* to go. The corridor was a dead end, and the only windows were heavily barred. They were trapped.

Eventually the guards managed to throw a huge net over the wolf, forcing him slowly to the ground. Once the Big Bad Wolf was tied up, Mayor Fitch stepped forward.

'So, here we all are again!' he exclaimed. 'This is quite the reunion! Still, at least now you can see that I've won. *I'm* in control and *nothing* that you or anyone else can do is going to change that!' His face had twisted up into a sneer, which he rearranged, putting on a fake, kindly smile.

'Now *you*,' Fitch said, jabbing a stubby finger towards the jailer. 'Lock them up and throw away the key! We shall have to think of a suitable punishment for our most *heroic* rebels. Banishment won't quite cut the mustard this time. We need something a bit more . . . *extreme*, don't you think?'

His guards cackled as they dragged the children and the Big Bad Wolf into the cell with Hansel and Gretel. The jailer slammed the door shut, locked it, bolted it, drew the heavy wooden bars across, and then threw the keys out of the window.

'What on earth did you do *that* for?' barked Fitch.

'What, sir?' asked the guard, looking confused.

'Why did you do that with the keys?'

'Er, you told me to, sir,' protested the guard.

'It's just a saying,' groaned Fitch, rubbing his forehead wearily. 'Very well . . . Guards!'

Three of his bodyguards ran forward.

'Arrest this man, put him on the banishment boat with the others.'

Fitch shook his head in irritation. At this rate, it wouldn't be long before he'd have to banish the whole town. He was just starting to wonder what would happen if he *did* have to banish the whole town when there was a loud scream from outside.

'Trolls!' screamed first one voice and then loads more. 'There's a troll invasion!'

There was the chilling sound of hundreds of rhythmically thudding footsteps and then metal striking hard against metal.

Fitch grinned, and then whispered, 'So . . . it begins!'

10

The Battle for Tale Town

*A*s the battle for Tale Town raged on, one figure stood calmly in front of the Story Tree. It was the troll leader Hurrilan. He looked across as one of the giants managed to pick up an entire platoon of Fitch's guards and throw them one by one into the Tale Town river. The minotaurs were charging around creating chaos in whichever direction their horns pointed, and Humpty Dumpty was sitting on top of a very narrow-looking wall, throwing sticks, stones and insults down on to Mayor Fitch's army.

'You have a face like an elbow!' he cackled out gleefully as he dropped a particularly big log on one unfortunate guard.

'Your shoes don't suit you!' he shouted as he prepared to drop something else, then lost his balance and tumbled off the wall, to land with a crunch on the floor.

'Oh dear . . .' he groaned. 'Can someone fetch me a new shell please?'

Hurrilan waved his hand through the air and a new shell magically appeared around Humpty Dumpty.

'*Wow!*' said Humpty Dumpty, looking surprised. 'Thanks!'

'Just be more careful next time!' said Hurrilan, then turned his attention back to the magical branches that spread out above him. He smiled despite the chaos. *Finally* he was here . . . He could actually touch the Story Tree!

Softly Hurrilan whispered a short story beneath his breath and marvelled as a small silver shoot grew out of the tree. His finger ran along the shoot as it unfurled into a delicate leaf, and instantly he was transported into the

world of the story he had just told — as if he were *actually* there.

He knew that this would happen, of course. *Everyone* knew how the Story Tree worked. It was just that he'd never seen it for himself.

B u t there it was! The first troll story in over two hundred years was now growing on the tree – just as it *ought* to be. Just as it *had* been when the trolls and the humans had first planted the Story Tree, all those years ago.

Hurrilan looked up at his story on the tree and smiled again, but was distracted by the sound of a spear zipping past his head. He spun around. There would be all the time in the world to explore the wonders of the Story Tree . . . *later*.

First there was a battle to win.

He turned to face Fitch's army and ran towards them, brandishing the gnarled wooden

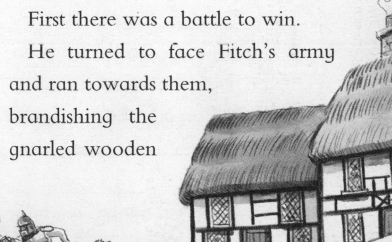

staff with the red crystal on top that gave him most of his power. Wherever he pointed the crystal, huge bolts of energy shot out, turning soldiers to stone, or birds, or plants – and in some cases, nothing at all.

———————◆◆———————

'We have to get out of here, *now*,' urged Hefferson as he ushered Fitch down the secret tunnel that led out of the palace, beyond the new wall.

'Yes,' agreed Fitch. 'You're right. It's just . . . you know, *the plan*!'

'Well . . .' replied Hefferson, 'unless that plan involves you being turned into stone by one of those trolls, then we'd better rethink it!'

He pulled Fitch along by the arm

as they hurried down the tunnel after the rest of the Mayor's bodyguards.

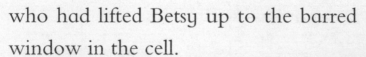

'What's happening out there?' demanded Jack, who had lifted Betsy up to the barred window in the cell.

'**WhaAaa Aaaaaat!**'squawked Betsy, sounding shocked.

'The trolls have won?' gasped Anansi. 'Fitch's men have *all* been captured?'

'**WhaAaaaat!**' said Betsy again, frowning.

'I *know* that's what you just said,' replied Anansi. 'It's just that I can't believe it.' They all fell silent for a moment. It was *obvious* that Mayor Fitch wasn't fit to rule Tale Town. He'd done an awful lot of *really* bad things, and that was *before* you included his plan to introduce a ten-hour-long school day, but even so . . . Was Tale Town *now* going to be ruled by Hurrilan? How was *that* going to be any better?

'WhaAaaaat!' added Betsy excitedly.

'Quartz is there too, so –' said Hansel eagerly.

'– perhaps he can help us?' continued Gretel.

Just then Red's mirror pinged. She flipped it open,

'Quartz! You've *got* to help us!' she exclaimed. 'We're trapped in a cell and . . .' The view in the mirror suddenly changed as Quartz's face slid out of view and another face replaced it. Hurrilan's face.

'*I see . . .*' he said. 'So *this* is how Tale Town always seemed to know my plans. You had a little spy!'

'No! It wasn't like that!' insisted Red. 'Quartz was just—'

'Betraying me!' interrupted Hurrilan.

Then his image faded and the mirror only showed Red's worried face.

'I think that went pretty well, all things considered!' said Jack hopefully.

'WhaAaaaaat!' said Betsy quietly.

'No, you're right,' replied Jack. 'We're *doomed*!'

'That means Hurrilan's going to be looking for us,' said Wolfie.

Hansel and Gretel nodded.

'We need to —'

'— get out of here!' they added.

'Great idea!' sneered the Big Bad Wolf, who had eventually chewed himself free of the net. 'But if you hadn't noticed, we're locked in and the keys got chucked out of the window!'

'Hmm . . .' said Rapunzel, smiling as she untied her hair. '*However* will we get them back?' Seconds later her hair was cascading out of the small window. 'This is *literally* the oldest trick in the book!' she said as her hair reached the floor. She gave her plaits a flick, and the ends wrapped around the keys and tied themselves into a neat little bow. Then she smiled, pulled the keys up,

walked over to the door and
unlocked it.

The Big Bad Wolf whistled
between his teeth. '*Impressive*! If
you kids ever want to come
out huntin' with me, then
you're welcome any time, *and*
you can have your pick of the
trophy – heads or tails.'

'What do you mean, "heads
or tails"?' asked Cole.

'Don't ask . . .' groaned
Wolfie. 'Dad, why don't you

get that wooden beam out of the way?'

'Right you are,' said the wolf happily as he heaved the huge bar out of the way as if it was made of cardboard.

Soon they were running through the passages of the castle. The battle outside was over and the trolls were celebrating in the Market Square, all completely fascinated by the Story Tree. Anansi peered through one of the windows and found a route that looked clear.

'This way!' he said, pointing out the route. 'From there we can make our way into the woods and head back to the hideout without anyone seeing us.'

'But w h a t *then*?' asked Jack. 'I mean, it looks like Fitch has gone and Hurrilan's in charge now. But what about everyone else? What about all the townsfolk? What's going to happen to them?'

'There's *nothing* we can do about that right now,' said Red. 'There aren't enough of us, and *besides*, you know what Hurrilan's like – he thinks we're on Fitch's side. We need to wait until everything's calmed down a bit before we speak to him, otherwise it's just—'

'Otherwise it's just *what*?' asked a cold voice from the end of the corridor. It was Hurrilan.

Everyone stood very still, apart from Jack who bent down and picked Betsy up, whispering something quietly as he did so.

Nobody spoke as a group of five armed trolls came slowly closer. When they were about five metres away, Jack spun around and helped Betsy flap out of the window.

'What was that?' demanded Hurrilan.

'I think it was a bird,' replied one of the trolls.

'Really?' said Hurrilan. 'It's going to take a lot more than a bird to get you out of *this*.'

11

Troll Town?

'The last time I saw any of *you*,' said Hurrilan, 'was after I had taken you in, given you shelter, warmth, food . . .' He looked at the children sharply as his soldiers led them through the town towards their makeshift prison by the riverbank. 'Of course, that was *before* I knew you had betrayed me. That *Rufaro* had betrayed me.'

'It wasn't like that!' protested Anansi. 'My Uncle Rufaro was—'

'Oh, I *know* what your uncle was doing!' spat Hurrilan furiously. 'Plotting with Mayor Fitch! I just feel a fool for not realizing sooner! Anyway, don't you worry. Rufaro and your mother are perfectly safe –' he tapped the crystal on the top of his staff – 'trapped in *here*.'

'Hurrilan!' called out a tall water troll as she hurried over. 'Some of the humans are trying to leave their houses now that the fighting has stopped.'

'They will remain inside,' said Hurrilan curtly. 'Place an armed watch on each house. Until we can tell who's on Fitch's side and who isn't, it's not safe to allow them out.' He glared at Anansi. 'And it's *very* hard to tell who's on Fitch's side. *Isn't it?*'

'But my uncle *wasn't* on Fitch's side!' protested Anansi. 'He was helping us to get Quartz back home. He was trying to *help* you! Fitch's men followed us. It was *them* who lied, not my uncle!'

'Yes, yes, I'm sure,' Hurrillan said impatiently. 'But that doesn't explain why you were all safe and sound, hiding away in Fitch's palace during the battle.'

'We'd been captured!' protested Red. 'We were *prisoners*!'

'You didn't look like prisoners to me,' spat Hurrilan.

'We'd escaped!' said Ella.

'How *convenient*.' Hurrilan turned to the troll on his right. 'Make sure they're, securely locked up, but separate them first – they're *very* resourceful.' He turned to walk off when there was a dramatic, squawky splash from the river next to them.

A very wet, *very* cross Betsy splashed up through the water, glared at Hurrilan and shrieked, '*WHAAAAAA AAAATTTTTT!*'

'Of course! The talking hen,' said Hurrilan, kneeling down close to Betsy. 'So . . . what *exactly* makes you think that I should set them free?'

'**WhaAaaaaAaaaaat!**' said Betsy gravely.

'You have proof that they're telling the truth?' Hurrilan paused for a moment. 'Very well, I shall indulge you. Where is this proof?'

There was another splash as Lily also swam up to the riverbank.

'*Here!*' she exclaimed, holding out the

secret Story Tree branch that she had been growing down in her cave. '*This* will explain everything!'

Hurrilan stood there for a moment, a look of awe on his face.

'Is that a cutting from . . . *the Story Tree?*' he asked. 'How did you get it?'

'Ah, yes . . .' said Wolfie hesitantly. 'Well, that's kind of a long story.'*

Hurrilan bent closer to the plant. 'And you managed to cultivate it?'

'Yes,' exclaimed Lily. 'It's been easy! I'm a *totally* brilliant gardener!'

Hurrilan smiled ever so slightly. 'Well, that *is* good news,' he said. 'I *shall* listen to what you have to say. But mark my

---

* It's a long story you can read in *The Magic Looking Glass*. You'll like it.

words, if this is a trick, you will all pay the most serious price imaginable.'

'Detention?' gasped Jack.

Hurrilan looked confused. 'No! Worse than detention!'

'You don't mean . . . no pudding – *ever again?*'

'*What?* No! I mean The. Most. Serious. Price. *Imaginable.*'

'Having to wear pants made of something really scratchy with the label still in them?'

'Oh, *forget it!*' Hurrilan shook his head. 'But this had better *not* be a trick!'

Then he reached out, and lightly touched the tiny silver tree . . .

Hurrilan found himself immersed in a whole world of

stories. Some of them he recognized, but he'd never seen them from *this* angle. He saw himself and his old friends Rufaro and Adeola embracing, after not seeing each other for decades. He saw how happy it had made Rufaro. He saw the sadness on Anansi's face when his uncle and his mother, Adeola, were trapped inside the magic crystal. He saw the truth about Mayor Fitch, and how Rufaro had never been anything but Fitch's enemy; how, over the years, Fitch

had been lying to manipulate the people of Tale Town into fearing the trolls. And he saw the children – Red, Jack, Anansi and all their friends – fighting against that fear in any way they could.

At last Hurrilan knew that Fitch had been lying all along. As the world of the Story Tree faded away, he looked around at the expectant faces.

'I'm sorry,' he said quietly, turning to Anansi. 'You *were* telling the truth, and so was your uncle. I promise, as soon as we have this situation under control, I'll free him and Adeola.'

'*NOW!*' screamed a voice from the top of the half-built wall that surrounded Tale Town. 'Turn it on *now!*'

Jack spun round to see Fitch on the wall, surrounded by his bodyguards and hundreds more soldiers.

'Defensive positions!' yelled Hurrilan, grabbing his magical staff, but he was too late. A crackling buzz filled the air as the whole wall vibrated with power. Strips of metal that ran along the stone began to glow – a dim, hesitant light that increased in waves until it was soon blinding. The whole wall was glowing, pulsing with an energy that seemed thick, solid and heavy enough to make

Jack's head ache. But if it made *his* head ache, it was doing something *much* worse to the trolls. He watched as they fell to their knees groaning, or leaned back against nearby walls, too weakened to even stand. The trolls looked at each other, eyes wide with panic and worry. Something was wrong. Something was *very* wrong.

Without warning, bright bolts of light came bursting out of the small brass circles in the wall. One struck the staff in Hurrilan's hand, sending it flying. He had to dive out of the way of another that nearly hit him full in the chest. Each bolt of light struck a different troll, knocking them off their feet and leaving them dazed on the floor. Jack watched as one troll scrambled up and tried angrily to use her magic. The look of horror on her face when nothing happened was awful.

'There's *nothing* you can do!' Fitch shouted. 'Now *I* have control of all your magic! And just *imagine* what I can do with it. Whole cities built in a moment, whole armies destroyed at the wave of my hand! To think that you had *all that power* and you did nothing with it. It's pathetic!'

'*No*,' shouted Hurrilan. 'To have all that power and not *abuse* it. That's real strength!'

'It doesn't look like that from up

here!' Fitch laughed as a bolt of light shot down, crashing into Hurrilan, throwing him backwards to lie still on the dirt.

12

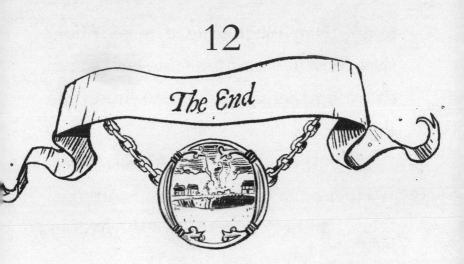

The End

*F*itch clambered down from the wall. In one hand he carried a small wooden box with a brass barrel on the front, which he held out threateningly as he marched into Market Square.

'It's over, you hear? *Over!*' barked Fitch, looking down in disgust at Hurrilan, sprawled on his back beneath the Story Tree.

'You see your leader?' he shouted

to the assembled trolls. 'Lying there, *helpless*? When he wakes up, he'll swear an oath to serve *me*. To do whatever I say.'

'He'll never do it,' said Anansi.

'He'll have to,' said Fitch, smirking, 'if he wants to save the lives of every troll here.'

'But why do you hate the trolls so much?' yelled Red.

'Why do you *not*?' asked Fitch. 'They're *different*. They're not like *us*! They're a threat!'

'No,' said Red. '*You're* the threat. And we're not anything like *you*!'

148

Fitch smiled.
'I always knew
there would be a
few sympathizers,
but that's no
problem. After all, *I*
control the Story Tree.
I can plant whatever
stories I like on there and they
become the truth! Have you never
heard the phrase "History is written by
the victors"?'

'I have . . .' said Hurrilan as he rose
unsteadily to his feet. 'But what makes
you so certain that you'll win?'

Fitch laughed out loud, and tossed a
stone to land at Hurrilan's feet. 'Go on
then,' he sneered, looking around at the

crowd. 'Turn *that* into something. How about a bunch of flowers? Admit it!' crowed Fitch, turning back to Hurrilan. 'You can't do it, *can you?*'

Hurrilan shook his head. 'No,' he admitted. '*I* can't.'

'You've lost all your magic!' taunted Fitch. 'Just like the rest of them.' He gestured at the trolls being chained up around the square. 'So how on earth do you think you can win? Let me demonstrate!'

He raised the box in his hand and swung it round to aim it at one of his guards. The guard nervously stepped backwards as Fitch pressed the button. The box shone with a bright light, just as the wall had done, then there was a

flash, and suddenly Fitch was standing next to a statue of a very surprised-looking guard.

'You see the power I have *now*?' he asked, his eyes gleaming.

As all this was happening, Hurrilan gestured ever so slightly towards his staff, which lay on the ground a few metres away. Betsy noticed and nodded back. Her eyes narrowed, and then she loudly squawked out, **'WhaAaaaat!'**

There was a burst of action. Hansel and Gretel darted towards the guards closest to them and grabbed the swords from their hands. Rapunzel flicked her hair out until it wrapped around the staff and yanked it over so that it came skidding to a halt at Hurrilan's

feet. Anansi made a clicking noise in the back of his throat, and within a few seconds, hundreds of spiders had appeared, scuttling up the legs of Fitch's guards and crawling all over them until they were scrabbling at their armour, trying to brush them off. The Big Bad Wolf barged into the guards near him, snapping at them with his sharp white teeth. Cole danced around in the air, performing whatever spells he could make up on the spot. Soon it was raining chocolate coins and Brussels sprouts while Jack, Ella and everyone else backed slowly away from Fitch.

Fitch looked amused. 'You think that this will help? The trolls have lost their magic and now *I* control it –

all of it! *This* is where it ends.'

'You're right!' yelled Hurrilan as he threw himself towards Fitch, the crystal on his staff glowing with a furious light. 'I can't use my *troll* magic, but I *can* use the magic in my staff! And yes, this *is* where it ends – for both of us!'

He spun the staff around them in one huge sweep. Bright trails of light flared out from the crystal, forming into thick, long ropes that flickered and whipped around them, as though held by huge, invisible hands. The light became too bright to see, the sound too loud to hear. Hurrilan and Fitch existed in the centre of a swirling red ball of light. With a rush the light shot outward at a terrifying speed, in an enormous wave of heat and noise.

Then it was gone.

There was a ringing sound in Jack's ears, and it took him a few seconds to realize that he had been thrown halfway across the square in some sort of explosion.

He looked around at the destroyed Market Square. A thick cloud of dust hung over everything, but even so, it was clear to see that Hurrilan, Fitch

and the Story Tree had gone. All that was left was a blackened, twisted shard of smoking wood that clawed up out of the deep crater where Fitch and Hurrilan had fought. What kind of magic could do something like *that*? What had happened to Hurrilan?

Jack picked himself up and peered down into the crater. What was that? It looked like some kind of movement . . .

There was a figure down there, clambering unsteadily to its feet, looking around in confusion. The figure climbed up the edge of the crater, growing clearer as they moved through the heavy dust that hung in the air. It was Rufaro.

More people ran forward and helped

Rufaro over the lip of the crater.

Rufaro looked around in confusion at the battle-scarred town.

'What *happened*?' he croaked.

Anansi was about to reply when he noticed someone else down in the crater. Another figure was stumbling out of the dust. He skidded down the side, hardly daring to believe his eyes. He knew that silhouette – he'd know it *anywhere*.

'Mum?' he called out, scrambling across the mud and rocks. '*Mum!*'

Then he had reached her and she pulled him into a tight hug as the dust settled all around them.

13

Happily Ever After

'Wow! That is *quite* some story!' said Alphege, the small green monkey, as he let go of the tiny leaf on the brand-new Story Tree that had been growing down in Lily's cave. It was now planted outside of Tale Town in a large clearing that *anybody* – human, troll, imp or otherwise – could use.

'I still can't believe I missed it all,' he

continued. 'You see, my second-favourite aunt makes the most *amazing* b a n a n a pie and she invited me over for tea, but, well . . . time ran away from us and I ended up staying a couple of days. It was all very nice, but sounds like you lot had *much* more fun!'

Jack looked at Red, who looked at Anansi, who looked round at all their other friends.

'**Whaaat**' growled Betsy under her breath.

'I'm not sure "fun" is exactly the right word . . .' began Anansi. 'Don't you remember the bit about Fitch locking us all up and turning the trolls into statues and stealing their magic?'

'Well, yes,' said Alphege, a bit dismissively, 'but you all got free, didn't you? And when Hurrilan cast the spell that transported him, the Story Tree and Fitch into the crystal from his staff, didn't that undo all Fitch's magic?'

'Well, yes, I suppose that *technically* it did,' replied Red.

'And when that happened, didn't all Fitch's men throw down their swords and run off? And once all your parents who'd been exiled to Far Far Away, or wherever it was, came home, I guess everything was pretty much back to normal?' said Alphege casually as he picked around under his armpit and eyed up the banana that Professor Hendricks was eating.

'Well . . . *yes*, but that's not the point!' exploded Red furiously. 'The point is that we risked *everything* to stop Fitch and . . .'

'And then it all turned out rather well!' finished Alphege, smiling. 'So shall we pop along to Greentop's Cafe? I *really* am rather peckish!'

As they all walked through Market Square, Ella was pleased to see grass shoots and flowers pushing up through the soil. The crater had been filled in and nearly all the repair work had been done to the houses that had been damaged in the battle. Most of the stone from Fitch's wall had been used for that, and now all that remained of it were a few broken blocks lying around.

'Hold on a minute!' boomed a loud voice. 'Where do you think *you're* going?'

Red spun around. 'Oh, hey, Rufaro!' she called out. 'Sorry, *Mayor* Rufaro.'

Anansi's uncle beamed. 'It's just been made official,' he said proudly, pointing at a small brass badge on his chest with the word 'Mayor' stamped into it.

'I can't think of anyone better for the job,' said Anansi.

'Thanks!' said Rufaro. 'So anyway, where *are* you going? Greentop's, right?'

'Yeah,' said Jack. 'Do you want to come too?'

'I'd love to,' said Rufaro, 'but I'm a busy man. Hurrilan's been on at me to do a few bits and pieces.'

'But . . . I thought Hurrilan and Fitch were trapped in the crystal on his staff? At least . . . that's what happened in the story,' said Alphege, looking confused.

Rufaro laughed. 'Well, yes, he *is*.'

He held up the crystal, which hung on a chain around his neck. It pulsed with a dancing red light. 'But he's found a way to come out of the crystal . . . at least, sort of. He always was good at magic — isn't that right, Hurrilan?'

There was a bright flash of red light as Hurrilan appeared in front of them. He looked thin and transparent, more like a projection of a person than an actual, solid thing.

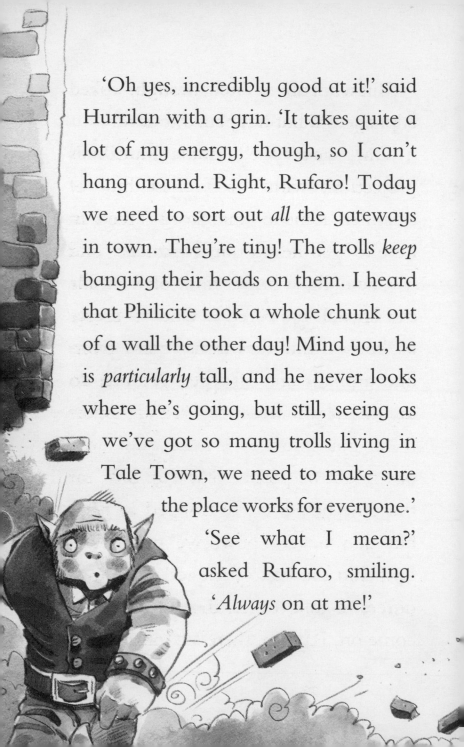

'Oh yes, incredibly good at it!' said Hurrilan with a grin. 'It takes quite a lot of my energy, though, so I can't hang around. Right, Rufaro! Today we need to sort out *all* the gateways in town. They're tiny! The trolls *keep* banging their heads on them. I heard that Philicite took a whole chunk out of a wall the other day! Mind you, he is *particularly* tall, and he never looks where he's going, but still, seeing as we've got so many trolls living in Tale Town, we need to make sure the place works for everyone.'

'See what I mean?' asked Rufaro, smiling. '*Always* on at me!'

'But what about Fitch, though?' asked Alphege. 'What happened to him?'

'Oh, he's *fine!*' said Hurrilan's projection, with the faintest hint of a smile. 'I mean, the Story Tree's in here too, so he's got plenty to do, and it's actually very comfortable inside the crystal — I've been able to create us houses and woodlands, and rivers and animals and all sorts! We can do anything we want to, really. Apart from, you know . . . *leave*. And even *that* might be possible *one day*. Still, for the time being, we're trapped in here, but you never know, we might end up being the best of friends! If he ever agrees to talk to me, that is! Anyway, come on, Rufaro, there's a lot to do.'

The projection of Hurrilan zipped back inside the crystal and Rufaro smiled at the children.

'I'd better be off,' he said. 'Have fun at Greentop's!'

<hr />

Jack sat back and looked around at his friends. *Everyone* was there. Even Lily had splashed up in the river near the cafe, so they'd put some picnic blankets out and were all sitting on the riverbank having their snacks.

Alphege and the gorillas were having musical milkshakes, and light tinkling melodies danced around through the trees. Cole was chasing after the musical notes, which you could just about see if you squinted out of the corner of your eye.

Hansel, Gretel, Wolfie and Ella had all chosen to have Alburtus Greentop's latest experiment, Burp-Bubble Pie. They sat there, each taking a few bites and burping up brightly coloured bubbles that drifted off through the air. When the bubbles finally popped they each made a huge belching sound.

The sun shone down warmly, and Jack smiled as the sound of the water mixed with the music and his friends' laughter. Lily had brought along a transformation spell, and Red, Rapunzel and Anansi were playing transform-a-tag with Quartz. Everybody laughed as Red got tagged and suddenly transformed into a giant squirrel in a bright red hood with a big bushy tail.

'You're *it*!' laughed Anansi as she spun around and tried to tag him back.

Jack sat there and watched it all. This was what they had fought so hard for – a happy, peaceful life, for *everyone*.

He looked over at Lily, who kept leaping out of the water, trying to do somersaults in mid-air and failing every time.

'WhaAaaaat!' squawked Betsy as a big splash of water cascaded over her.

'Oh, come on!' said Jack. 'I think she's getting better. One of these days she'll get the hang of it.'

Betsy shrugged, and then nestled in closer. As Jack patted the water off Betsy's back, she looked up at him and happily squawked, 'WhaAaaaat!'

Jack smiled. 'Yeah, you're right,' he said. 'Today *is* a good day!'

Then he lay back, with Betsy cradled in the crook of his arm, and thought about all the adventures that he and his

friends would be able to grow on the *new* Story Tree.

One thing was certain: the best was yet to come.

The End